Henry Copley Greene

**Théophile, a miracle play by Henry Copley Greene**

Henry Copley Greene

**Théophile, a miracle play by Henry Copley Greene**

ISBN/EAN: 9783743353077

Manufactured in Europe, USA, Canada, Australia, Japa

Cover: Foto ©Andreas Hilbeck / pixelio.de

Manufactured and distributed by brebook publishing software
(www.brebook.com)

Henry Copley Greene

**Théophile, a miracle play by Henry Copley Greene**

# THÉOPHILE
## A MIRACLE PLAY
### BY
## HENRY COPLEY GREENE

SCIRE

QVOD · SCIENDVM

BOSTON
SMALL, MAYNARD & COMPANY
MDCCCXCVIII

# PREFACE.

*The legend of Théophile's rebellion and re-pentance being common property, I have quarried in it without scruple, and have added from other legends the essential idea of this play, Théophile's fidelity to the Virgin.   Certain metaphors in her honor I have borrowed from the Rosa Mystica.   A few other phrases, including the sorcerer's "Hebrew," I have taken from the Miracle de Théophile of Ruteboeuf.  This quaint thirteenth-century play may be conveniently read in the version edited by Remy de Gourmont and published in Paris by the Mercure de France.*

H. C. G.

# CHARACTERS.

## IN THE PROLOGUE.

A Monk     *Thomas Wentworth Higginson.*

A Herald             *Katrine Coolidge.*

## IN THE PLAY PROPER.

The Virgin Mary
> *Eugenia Brooks Frothingham.*

Théophile          *Richard C. Cabot.*

Satan            *T. Russell Sullivan.*

Salatin          *Raphael Pumpelly.*

The Abbot Eusèbe
> *Thomas Wentworth Higginson.*

An Acolyte         *Katrine Coolidge.*

*The play was first performed, through the kindness of Mr. Joseph Lindon Smith, at the Teatro Bambino, in Dublin, New Hampshire, the 18th of July, 1898.*

# THÉOPHILE.

## THE PROLOGUE.

*Into a garden like the garden of an abbey there enter a* MONK *and a* HERALD. *And to those assembled to behold the play*

### THE HERALD *calls:*

Silence ; be silent, friends, and hark how we
    shall play
A wonder wrought by Her to whom the
    angels pray.

### THE MONK.

Brethren, entreat for us Our Blessed Lady's
    grace,
That we may set forth worthily before Her
    face
The trial of Her steadfast servant Théophile.
And bear ye patiently the ills we must re-
    veal,—
The secret sinful wiles of brother Mathurin,
The snares and mighty sorcery of Salatin,
Eusèbe the Abbot's wrath, and Satan's burn-
    ing rage,

[1]

And brother Théophile's impassioned will to
    wage
War against God; — bear all with faith in
    Heaven above,
And ye shall know a wonder of Our Lady's
    love.
Enough; but rest ye silent, though my words
    are done,
For now with song our Miracle shall be be-
    gun.

              [*They go out.*]

# SCENE I.

*The voice of* THÉOPHILE *is heard in song.*

Sir Guy the strong, Sir Guy the bold,
    Sir Guy whose soul shall never die,
        Lay dead within his coffin bark,
And fared with gifts of beaten gold
    Toward Arles where he was fain to lie.

But while a heaven-assaulting lark
    Sang gayly o'er the blessed Rhone,
        Three robbers waiting on the shore,
Men cursed with Cain's unholy mark,
    Seized on the knight who fared alone.

They saw and seized the gold he bore,
    Then cast him loose to drift from sight.
        He tarried sternly, fixed and cold;
And angels smote the robbers sore,
    And rescued all his offerings bright.

So strong Sir Guy, Sir Guy the bold,
    Sir Guy whose soul shall never die,
        Fared safe within his coffin bark,
Fared safe with all his gifts of gold
    To Arles, where he was fain to lie.

*Enter* THÉOPHILE.

Sooth, 't was a goodly miracle,

[3]

Proving Our Lady's power full well.
[*He makes the sign of the cross.*]
Praise alway to Her holy name.
And now what song? Again the same!
[*Sings.*]
*Sir Guy the strong, Sir Guy the bold,*
*Sir Guy whose soul shall never die —*


# SCENE II.

*Enter* EUSÈBE.

[*Threatening to strike* THÉOPHILE.]

Silence, blasphemer! Silence, treacherous
one!


THÉOPHILE [*in great anger*].

By God on high!
[*Restraining himself.*]
   Sweet Mother, aid thy son!


EUSÈBE.

Hold! Théophile, an thou dost love thy soul,
Call not on Heaven, lest eternal dole
O'erwhelm thee in thy black impenitence.

[4]

## THÉOPHILE.

Lord Abbot, in a moment's indolence
I sang, 't is true, but a right holy song,
Proving —

## EUSÈBE.

Think not to prove I do thee wrong.
I chide thee not for slight or seeming sin,
But damn thee, knowing thou hast sought to
    win
Infernal power from this Salatin,
Whose mighty sorcery —

## THÉOPHILE [*aside*].

Ah, Mathurin !
I see thy cunning and perfidious wiles !
[*Aloud.*]
Lord Abbot, trust not Mathurin's false smiles
And sugared words and sanctimonious
    sighs —

## EUSÈBE.

Ha ! What of him ?

## THÉOPHILE.

In deviltry he 's wise :
And knowing that I know what I do know,
He first accuseth me ! Is it not so ?

[5]

In vain dost thou impute to him thine evil
    thought,
For gentle Mathurin accuseth thee of nought !
Nay, in mute suffering memory he hid thy
    guilt
Even from God until his soul began to wilt
And utterly to wither in thy sin's fell heat.
Then, thrusting from him even innocent de-
    ceit,
Poor Mathurin did yield the knowledge of
    thy deeds
Unto the Virgin, telling all the while his
    beads,
And begging with such fervor thine escape
    from Hell
That I did hear him even in my distant cell !

THÉOPHILE.

Ye holy saints, may these things be —
Such craft, such deep duplicity —
    In this our world ?
Ah, sweet Saint John, give ear to me !
In Satan's pit right hastily
    Let him be hurled !

EUSÈBE.

Mad sinner, cease from raving. Listen si-
    lently.

[6]

I know that thou didst steal from the great
    treasury
The five tall golden goblets gone since
    Easter-morn.
Ah, better were 't for thee if thou hadst
    ne'er been born.

THÉOPHILE.
Is, then, my service, high in trust,
No weightier than mere breeze-blown
    dust ?

EUSÈBE.
Give here the keys !

THÉOPHILE.
Is my true steel so dark with rust
That for a liar's word I must
    Surrender these ?

EUSÈBE [*taking the keys*].
Yea, and thy greater sins wait greater pun-
    ishment.
For lustful crimes unspeakable thou shalt
    repent.

THÉOPHILE [*kneeling*].
Ah, Blessed Lady, sweet and fair,
Dear flower-like Virgin, hear my prayer,

[7]

And beg from God a wonder-sign
Proving that I am wholly Thine.

Eusèbe.

Despite this artful blasphemy I know thou art
Rebellious to Our Lady, cold, and black of
    heart,
A thief and lecherous, and eke a sorcerer,
Profaning to Hell's service service due to Her.

Théophile [*sings*].

"*Agios veris ros,*
   *Mai flos, audi nos !* "

Eusèbe.

[*Seizing the rosary from* Théophile's *hands.*]

Wherefore, fell Théophile, begone !  I cast
    thee forth
From out dear Saint Bernard's sweet fellow-
    ship.  Go North,
Go South, I reck not where; but flee for aye
    this place;
Yea, flee till thou hast met Our Lady face to
    face.

## SCENE III.

Théophile.

Belovèd Virgin, praise be to Thy name,
[*Kissing his medal.*]

[8]

And glory and eternal heavenly fame,
And my poor humble thanks that Thou hast
    made
Petition for me.

SALATIN [*aside, entering*].
            Théophile! Arrayed
In such disorder!

THÉOPHILE.
            Still She prays, I wot,
For my salvation.
[*Rising as he sees that the Abbot is no longer with him.*]
            But He hears Her not!
Ah, cold, high God, silent, implacable,
Wilt Thou not grant Christ's mother a mir-
    acle?
Canst Thou refuse Her? God, She kneels
    to Thee!
Saint John, ah, good Saint John, may this
    thing be?
        [*Going to the shrine of Saint John.*]
            *Johannes,*
"*Miserere mei et exaudi orationem meam!*"
            *Johannes, Johannes!*
Saint John, God heedeth not Our Lady's
    word!
Then pluck Him by the robe!

[9]

SALATIN [*aside*].
I 'll blight Christ's herd,
I 'll seize this lamb, if I am Salatin!

THÉOPHILE [*to Saint John*].
Thou *wilt* not? [*rising*] Then he 's like to
    Mathurin?
Yea, John is joined unto mine enemy,
And God Himself doth aid their enmity!
Ah, Thine injustice passeth tolerance!
Thou sendest me to wander throughout France
All penniless despite my trusty zeal
In serving Thy great servant.

SALATIN.
              Théophile!
Ho, Théophile! What ails thee?

THÉOPHILE [*not hearing*].
              Noxious snakes
Lisp out false charges, and the Abbot shakes
Condemning fingers in my face!

SALATIN.
              What ho!
My God, what anger! Soft, friend, soft and
    slow.
What ails thee? Speak. Mayhap with my
    poor aid —

[10]

THÉOPHILE [*still trembling with anger*].
And who art thou?

SALATIN.

Thy friend.   Be not dismayed.
I love thee very sweet, kind sir.   Speak, then.
Tell me thy griefs.

THÉOPHILE.

I ruled an hundred men,
The abbey serfs; I held the treasure-keys;
I paid out moneys, gathered all due fees
Even to-day, as during many years,
For my lord Abbot —

SALATIN.

My prophetic fears!
Thou art not dispossessed?

THÉOPHILE.

Yea, dispossessed,
And driven forth, goaded, harassed, distressed
Alike by men and Saints and God the King.
And though more sweetly than the angels
    sing
Our Lady prayed for me, God heeded not;
And cursèd John laughed loudly at my lot
When in the vulgar and the sacred tongue

[11]

I prayed his grace! Ah, could I but have flung
A gauntlet in his teeth! For I am done
With sufferance! Since God and Saints are one
In enmity against me, I 'll wage war,
Dread war, against their host.

SALATIN.

Soft, soft! Thou 'lt mar
Thy sure success! 'T is sure? Thou 'rt well prepared?

THÉOPHILE.

Nay, nay. God hideth where no man hath fared,
There, throned above the clouds, and neither spear
Nor wingèd shaft can find Him.
[*Shaking his fist.*]
Were He near —

SALATIN.

Beware His lightnings, friend!

THÉOPHILE.

I scorn their power!

[12]

Submit to God before the fatal hour
When —

THÉOPHILE.

Never unto Him ! Behold, kind sir,
Our Lady knelt and prayed. He looked on
    Her
And turned away. Ah! verily, my blood
Boils when I think on 't !

SALATIN.

       Stay ! In mire and mud
He 'll trample thee beneath His feet, if thus,
Alone, thou assailest Him. But join with
    us,
With me, sweet Théophile, and with my
    lord,
And thou shalt conquer, gaining a great
    hoard
Of treasure, wide fair lands, and many a
    slave.
Abbots shall do thy bidding : thou shalt pave
Thy palace-courts with gold —

THÉOPHILE.

       But tell me, friend,
Shall God's fell tyranny come to an end
In all the wondrous worlds ?

Yea, grievous shame,
Thou, Théophile, shalt bring upon His
name;
And thou shalt grow in conquering glorious
might
And rule the powers of day and darkling
night.
Yea, thou shalt be well-nigh omnipotent,
If thou wilt serve a king who is content
To lend thee aid.

THÉOPHILE.

Then bring me unto him.
Gladly I'll swear him fealty. Yea, each
whim
Of his shall be my law. Swift, swift, I pray,
Bring me to him.

SALATIN.

Be still; here is the way.
Thou seest yonder shaded mossy well,
Digged during ages when this gentle dell
Rang with the laughter of a water-sprite
And echoed with the wildest faun's delight?
There, when aloud strange magic words I
cry,
A form doth rise —

[14]

THÉOPHILE.

'T is Satan ?

SALATIN.

Yea, and I
Am Salatin !   Aha, thou fearest me ? —
Fear not, dear friend, I bear but love toward
    thee.
And my great lord is enemy to God.
    [*Slowly.*]
That evil God who gleefully hath trod
Thee, thee His faithful servant, under foot.

THÉOPHILE.

Enough, good Salatin, enough ; I 'll put
My hands between his hands : I 'll be his
    man !

SALATIN.

Right bravely said.  Thou fearest not the ban
Of Abbot or of Bishop or of Pope.

THÉOPHILE.

Nay, not if thou fulfillest my great hope !

SALATIN.

[*Drawing on the ground.*]
So.   Stand thou there, friend Théophile,

[15]

Until I call thee here to kneel
Before the king.
Watch how with mystic signs I deal:
Behold how stilly I must steal
Within the ring.

*[Kneeling before the open book and pointing with his
wand toward the homes of the four winds.]*

*Bagahi baca bacahé
Lamac cahi acabahé
Karrelyos.*

*[A great wind rages among the trees.]*

THÉOPHILE.

Salatin, dost thou not hear
An angel crying in great fear,

*[Chanting.]*

" *De profundis clamavi ad te, Domine* " ?

SALATIN.

The voice will cease.

*Lamac lamec bachalyos
Cabahagi sabalyos
Baryolos.*

*[There is a great noise of thunder.]*

THÉOPHILE.

The voice now draweth very near
And singeth gently in mine ear

[16]

*[Chanting.]*
" *Et ipse redimet Israel, ex omnibus iniquitatibus
    ejus.*"

SALATIN.

Sss! Hold thy peace!
*Lagazatha cabyolas
Samahac et famyolas
Harrahya!*
*[Red fire flares upward from the well.]*


# SCENE IV.

SATAN.

*[Rising, a trident in his hand.]*
Ho! Black thunderous bleak damnation!
Why this Hebrew incantation?
Hi! Is this thine adulation?
Worship me, weak Salatin.

THÉOPHILE [*coolly*].
Strange! He 's like to Mathurin!

SALATIN.

Kindest Satan,
Blessed Satan,
Let me greet thy Majesty!
Mighty Satan,
Glorious Satan,
Grant me —

[17]

#### SATAN.

Sss!   Whom do I see?

#### THÉOPHILE.

Théophile.

#### SATAN.

Mine enemy!

#### SALATIN.

Master, dark adversity
Makes him now thy willing friend.

#### THÉOPHILE.

Yea, to thee I 'll gladly bend,
If against the King on High
Thou wilt aid me.

#### SATAN.

That will I,
By my hate of Heaven's Lord!
Verily my flaming sword
Waits thy pleasure — S' death! Ha! Sss!
Salatin!

#### SALATIN.

Lord, what 's amiss?

#### SATAN.

Ah, slave, thou hast betrayed me with a kiss!

[18]

He 's still mine enemy.   Ho, devils, tss !
Hi, Salatin, but thou shalt roast for this ;
Yea, thou shalt sputter on the spit and hiss !

SALATIN.

O kindest Satan, blessed —

THÉOPHILE.

                Hold.   He 's true !
And thine injustice thou shalt dearly rue
If thou dost dare to damn him, innocent.

SALATIN [plaintively].

A saint I bring thee, cast forth indigent,
Despised, rejected, and condemned by God,
His master's Master —

THÉOPHILE.

              Yea, my feet had trod
The blood-stained rock of exile helplessly,
Had Salatin not brought me unto Thee.

SATAN.

Hoyo !   Thou wilt in sooth become my man ?

THÉOPHILE.

[*Kneeling on one knee and putting his hands between
the hands of Satan.*]

My Lord, I swear thee fealty !

[19]

SATAN.

All Hell can
For thee I 'll valiantly essay:
My huge might
Shall make the battle impish play:
And His plight
Shall be yet lower than thine to-day.
All this, my vassal, if thou 'lt solemnly for-
swear
Thy fealty to the Powers of the upper air!

SALATIN.

All, Théophile, if thou wilt solemnly forswear
Thy fealty to the Powers of the upper air!

THÉOPHILE [*rising*].

I will, and that right gladly!

SALATIN.

Dost thou then forswear
And utterly renounce thine enemy, the Father?

THÉOPHILE.

I do forswear [*the wind wails*] and utterly
renounce the Father.

SATAN.

'T is well.

[20]

THÉOPHILE.
So help me Hell!

SALATIN.
Dost thou forswear and utterly renounce the
Son?
THÉOPHILE.
I do forswear and utterly renounce the Son.
[*Low thunder rumbles in the air.*]

SATAN.
'T is well.

THÉOPHILE.
So help me Hell!

SALATIN.
And dost thou utterly renounce the Holy
Ghost?
THÉOPHILE.
Yea, I do utterly renounce the Holy Ghost.
[*It thunders furiously.*]

SATAN.
'T is very well.

THÉOPHILE.
So help me Hell!

[21]

**SALATIN.**

Finally thou dost forswear the Virgin Mother
of God?

[THÉOPHILE *stands silent, quaking.*]

Speak.   Dost thou utterly forswear the
Mother of God?

**THÉOPHILE.**

Nay!

**SALATIN.**

Nay?   But, Théophile —

**SATAN.**                          .

Be still.— Sweet servitor,
Lo, thou shalt be a prince, a king, an em-
peror,
If thou 'lt renounce the Virgin's name; if
not, forever
Thy soul shall groan in nethermost Hell.
Renounce Her!

**THÉOPHILE.**

Never!

**SALATIN.**

Art mad?

**SATAN.**

Be still.—

[22]

Renounce Her, or thy corpse shall lie
Dead there! But thy poor tortured soul
shall never die!

THÉOPHILE [*falling on his knees*].

Hail to Thee, Mother whom men and angels
love!

SALATIN [*hastening away*].

Master, beware. He prays to Her above!

THÉOPHILE.

Red rose glowing through life's gloom,
  Lily of virginity,
Violet in Thy tender bloom,
  Wind-flower of humility,
Rosemary whose balm-like breath
  Wafts to all souls clemency,
Save me from the jaws of death!
  Lily of virginity,
Save me from the jaws of death!

SATAN.

Ha ha! Ha ha ha!
She rejects thee proudly!
Ha ha! Hi hi hi!
Then renounce Her loudly,

[23]

Or thou shalt surely die — I warn thee now
   afresh —
And serpents with red fangs of fire shall rend
   thy flesh !

THÉOPHILE.

Virgin, flower of eglantine,
   Rescue me from Satan's ire !
Rose of Heaven, my soul is Thine ;
   Save it from eternal fire !

SATAN.

Curs'd Théophile, renounce Her, or thou
   diest !

THÉOPHILE.

Dear Virgin, glory to Thee in the highest !

SATAN.
[*Holding his right hand aloft with power.*]
Then die, perfidious heavenly one !

THÉOPHILE [*sore woundea*].

Dearest Lady, hear Thy son !
   Flower of eglantine, red rose,
Lily fair, glad life is done :
   Through eternal fiery woes
I must suffer for my sin,
   Suffer far, oh, far from Thee !

[24]

Ere my punishment begin
   Pity, then, ah pity me:
Grant me one sweet parting grace,
   One dear vision of Thy face!

SATAN.

Hi hi! Ha ha ha! Hi hi! Ha ha!

THÉOPHILE [*faintly*].

Ah, flower of eglantine, red rose,
   Sweet violet, smile upon my woes,
Grant me one sight of Thy dear face!
   [*Dying.*]
Oh, may I ne'er behold Thy grace?

SATAN.

Ho ha! Ha hi!
[*To the devils below.*]
*Lagazatha cabyolas*
*Samahac et famyolas.*
*Harrahya!*

## SCENE V.

*The voice of* OUR LADY:
Peace, peace be with thee, Théophile.

SATAN [*hastily*].
*Ha, lamac lamec bachalyos.*

[25]

OUR LADY [*appearing*].
Thy love hath saved thee, Théophile.

SATAN [*in great rage*].
*Hi, cabahagi sabalyos*
*Baryolos !*
[*He descendeth into Hell.*]

OUR LADY.
Dread wound of Théophile,
Close, close and heal :
Red blood of Théophile,
Soft onward steal :
Dear soul of Théophile,
Leave woe for weal :
Fear not, sweet Théophile —
[OUR LADY *doth bless his forehead with a kiss.*]

THÉOPHILE.
Dear Lady, flower of eglantine,
I fear no longer Satan's ire :
Red rose of Heaven, all joy is mine ;
My soul shall sing, yea, in Hell-fire.

OUR LADY.
Night shall not seize thee, Théophile.
Nay, God will deal
Righteously toward thee, Théophile.

[26]

Win but the love that He doth feel
    For thee : yea, kneel
In trust to Him.   To Him appeal
As unto me, my Théophile —
God bless thee, blessed Théophile.

[*She is gone.*]


## SCENE VI.

### Théophile.

Red rose glowing through life's gloom,
    Lily of virginity,
Violet in Thy tender bloom,
    Wind-flower of sweet sanctity,
Rosemary whose balm-like breath
    Fills me with humility,
Thine am I, e'en unto death ;

But for Thee and for Thy love
    [*Rising.*]
Praise unto Thee, great God above !
Yea, praise to Thee and endless fame,
    [*Kissing his medal.*]
And honor, Lady, to Thy name !
  [*Walking toward the abbey, he sings.*]
    "*Ave maris stella*,
      *Dei Mater alma*,

[27]

*Atque semper virgo,*
*Felix coeli porta . . .*

"*Virgo singularis,*
*Inter omnes mitis,*
*Nos culpis solutos,*
*Mites fac et castos . . .*

"*Sit laus Deo Patri,*
*Summo Christo decus,*
*Spiritui Sancto,*
*Tribus honor unus.*"

EUSÈBE.

[*As a simple monk, entering joyously, followed by an acolyte bearing the mitre.*]

Ah, Théophile !

THÉOPHILE.

Once more I seek this place
For I have met Our Lady face to face.
[*With bowed head.*]
But, driven guiltless from the abbey door,
I sought with Salatin to wage a war
'Gainst God —

EUSÈBE [*kneeling*].
Dear Théophile !

THÉOPHILE [*raising him*].
My Lord —

[28]

EUSÈBE.

Be still.

[*Taking the mitre and setting it upon his head.*]

Forgiven is thy sin ; and 't is Our Lady's will
That in obedience unto thee thy lord shall
    bow
And set the mitre reverently upon thy brow.
For, saith Our Lady, thy strong hand shall
    wield
The crozier, while I hold the keys which I
    did yield
To thine accuser —

THÉOPHILE.

Mathurin ?

EUSÈBE.

Yea, even so,
But he is dead.

THÉOPHILE [*crossing himself*].

Poor Mathurin !

EUSÈBE.

Mourn not ; for lo,
Dear Théophile, the Lord our God is very
    just
And full of equity ; in Him we 'll put our
    trust ;

[29]

And though He chasteneth us, we'll give
    Him endless praise.
Praise Him ; yea, praise Him, brethren ; laud
    His holy ways !

ALL [sing].

" *Te Deum laudamus : te Dominum confitemur.*
*Te aeternum Patrem omnis terra veneratur.*
*Tibi omnes angeli, tibi coeli, et universae potestates.*
*Tibi cherubim et seraphim incessabili voce po-*
    *clamant :*
*Sanctus, sanctus, sanctus, Dominus Deus Sabaoth.*
*Pleni sunt coeli et terra, majestatis gloriae tuae.*

THÉOPHILE.

" *Benedicamus Patrem et Filium, cum Sancto*
    *Spiritu.*

ALL.

" *Laudamus et super-exaltemur in saecula.*
    *Amen.*"

# EPILOGUE.

Well chanted.— Now, dear friends, our Miracle is done.
Then if, by some far greater miracle, we 've
  won
Your hearts, lend us your hands ; clap gladly,
  every one !

*Théophile, a Miracle Play, by Henry Copley Greene, was printed from type at the Everett Press in Boston for Small, Maynard & Company of Boston, in December, 1898, in an edition of two hundred and fifty copies, on Alton Mills handmade paper.*

*The frontispiece was reproduced from a painting, representing a scene in the play, by Cecilia Beaux.*

www.ingramcontent.com/pod-product-compliance
Lightning Source LLC
Chambersburg PA
CBHW061239260626
47172CB00003B/922

* 9 7 8 3 7 4 3 3 5 3 0 7 7 *